BISCUIT BEAR

MINI GREY

RED FOX

Our story starts with a lump of pastry that Horace's Mum gave him,

LOUR

The Golden Bun
FOR BISCUIT LOVERS EVERYWHERE
CAKES • BUNS • TARTS

which Horace would usually
roll about over the floor
and furniture

until

it was

deep grey

and **fluffy**

(and quite a lot smaller).

But today

Horace's Mum gave him
a biscuit cutter in the shape of
a bear to use.

Horace stamped out a pastry bear
and gave it currant eyes and a nose.

Horace's Mum put it in the oven to cook.

Twenty minutes later the biscuit bear was golden-coloured and smelt lovely, and Horace wanted to take a bite *but –*

An hour later Horace remembered the cooled biscuit bear and was about to take a bite *but –*

"No, Horace," said Horace's Mum, "it is too hot. You must wait for it to cool down."

Before bedtime

Horace thought of the golden biscuit bear and he was just gazing at it, but –

"No, Horace,"

said Horace's Mum, "you have just cleaned your teeth."

"No, Horace," said Horace's Mum, "you are just about to have dinner. You will spoil your appetite."

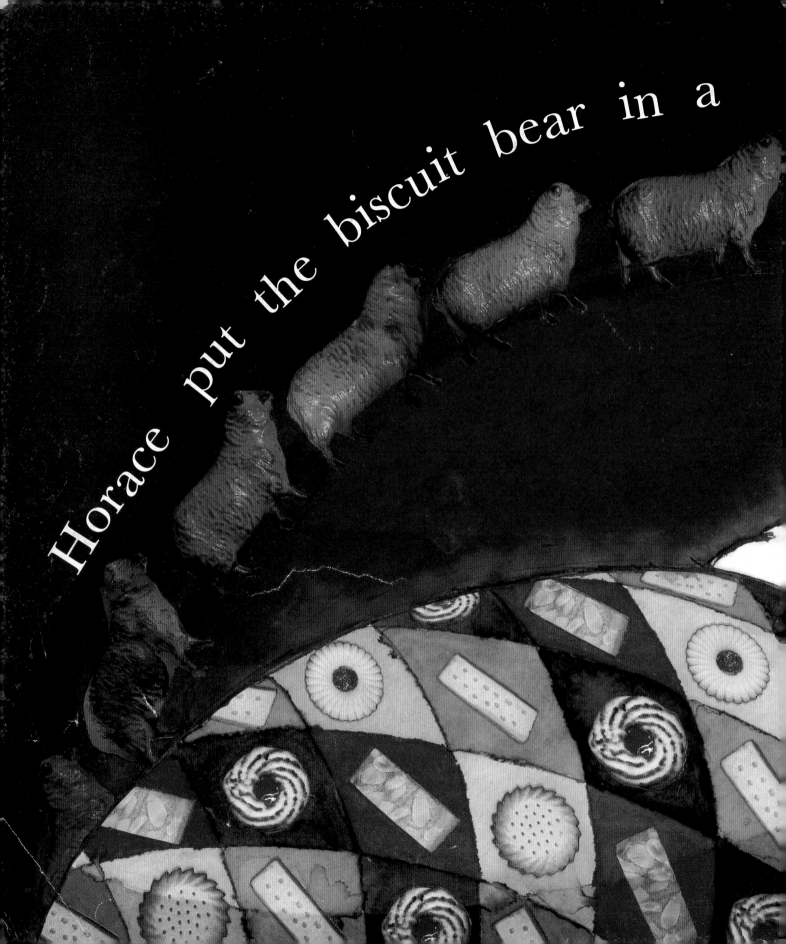

Horace put the biscuit bear in a

little tin, and put it on his pillow.

It was the
middle of the night.
Biscuit Bear woke up.
He yawned and stretched,
and looked about for
somebody to play with.
Everyone seemed
to be asleep.

Biscuit Bear had an idea.
I shall **make** some friends,
he said to himself,
and went to the **kitchen**.

Biscuit Bear found **butter** and **flour** and **milk.**

He **mixed** up a mixture, and **rolled** it and **shaped** it, and put the first batch of friends in the oven to cook.

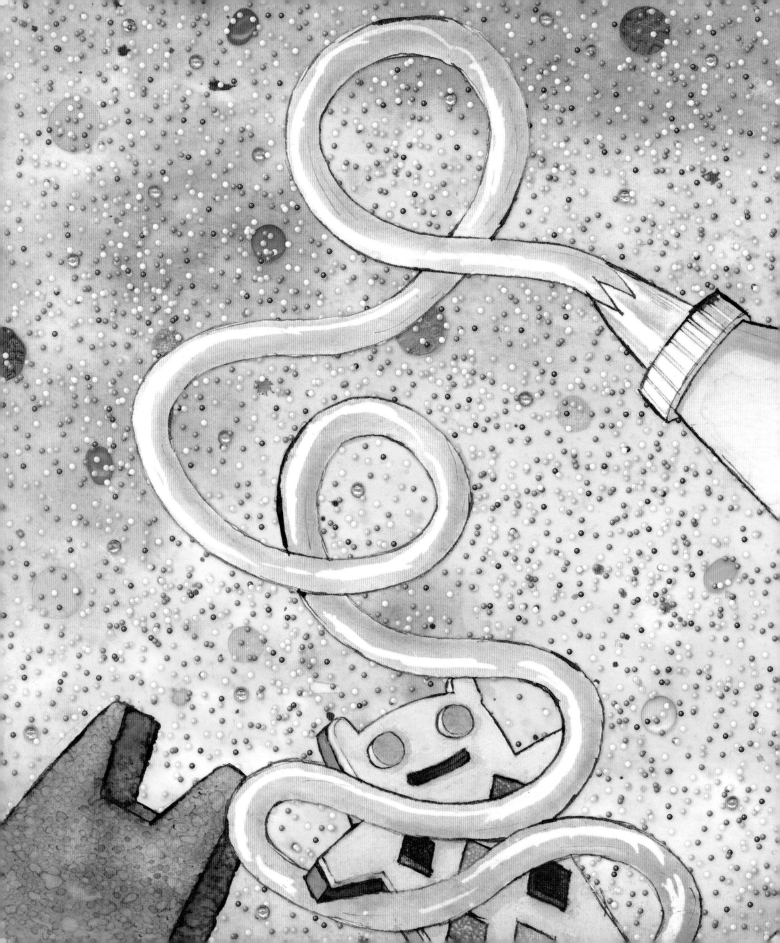

When they had cooled,
Biscuit Bear dressed them in
icing of many colours,
hundreds and thousands,
and **candied peel** and *glacé* cherries
and little silver balls.

"And now,"
Biscuit Bear said
to his new friends,
"let the fun begin!"

Roll Up! Roll Up!

One night only!
Biscuit Bear's Circus is
performing in
the kitchen!

Watch the Acrobats
as they
toss and tumble!

Gasp as the Strongbear raises the rolling pin!

Scream with surprise as our Aeronaut is fired from the ketchup bottle!

The circus was so exciting
that no one noticed
the **shadow** looming
in the doorway.

Bongo the Dog liked biscuits.
(But not in a way that is
necessarily good
for the
biscuits.)

Biscuit Bear **just** managed to clamber to safety.

Biscuit Bear looked sadly at the mess.
He suddenly realized
that he needed to find
a place where a biscuit
could be safe.

When Horace awoke the **next morning,**
he reached for the tin
that had contained the little biscuit bear,

Horace

but all he found was crumbs,
and a card
that looked
familiar.

The life of a biscuit
is usually **short** and *sweet*,
but Biscuit Bear has found
somewhere safe to be.

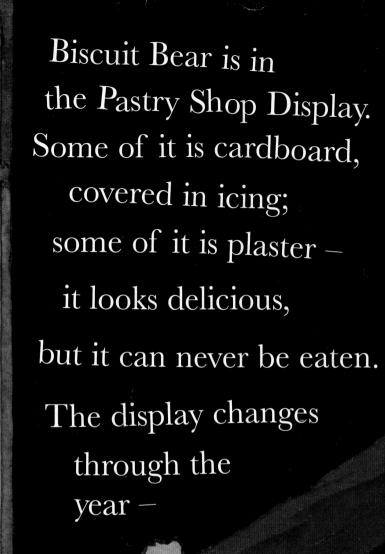

Biscuit Bear is in
the Pastry Shop Display.
Some of it is cardboard,
covered in icing;
some of it is plaster –
it looks delicious,
but it can never be eaten.

The display changes
through the
year –

but Biscuit Bear is
always the **star;**
spring, summer
and winter.

More delicious treats from Mini Grey:

Egg Drop
The Pea and the Princess
Traction Man is Here
The Adventures of the Dish and the Spoon

Dedicated to

Jo

(and to biscuit lovers everywhere)

BISCUIT BEAR
A RED FOX BOOK 978 0 099 45108 2

First published in Great Britain by Jonathan Cape,
an imprint of Random House Children's Books
A Random House Group Company

Jonathan Cape edition published 2004
Red Fox edition published 2005

9 10

Copyright © Mini Grey, 2004

The right of Mini Grey to be identified as the author of this work has been asserted
in accordance with the Copyright, Designs and Patents Act 1988.

All rights reserved.

Red Fox Books are published by Random House Children's Books,
61–63 Uxbridge Road, London W5 5SA

www.**kids**at**randomhouse**.co.uk
www.**rbooks**.co.uk

Addresses for companies within The Random House Group Limited can be found at:
www.randomhouse.co.uk/offices.htm

THE RANDOM HOUSE GROUP Limited Reg. No. 954009

A CIP catalogue record for this book is available from the British Library.

Printed in Singapore